With Best Wishes!
Rosemary & Paul Volpp

The HAPPY-est Bear

A Biography

By Rosemary and Paul Volpp

PUBLISHED IN THE UNITED STATES OF AMERICA
BY
BLACK FOREST PRESS
P.O.Box 6342
Chula Vista, CA 91909-6342
1-800-451-9404
First Edition, First Printing
August, 2001

Thank you P.A. for all your help!

A percentage of the proceeds from the sales of this book will be donated to the Elizabeth Glaser Pediatric AIDS Foundation. www.pedAIDS.org

The pictures of Happy at her news conference at John F. Kennedy Airport are courtesy of *Teddy Bear and Friends* magazine.©

Printed in China
Library of Congress
Cataloging-in-Publication

ISBN: 1-58275-061-0

Dedication...

To Paul, for asking me to say "I do."
To daughter Rosemary and her Ron; to son PA and his Teri;
To grandchildren, Ad, Amanda, and Jess;
Brian and his Heather, Andrew and Angela;
To my late mother, who sewed a fine seam;
To Happy's "Auntie," Pam Hebbs - in memoriam.

And for all the wondrous adventures she caused us to experience,
to the teddy bear we call Happy Anniversary.

She set a world–record—*BUT*…
That wasn't what *really* mattered.

Prologue

During the last half of the 1990's, the world of arctophiles (teddy bear collectors) became immune to the astronomical high prices fetched by bears at auction. Such was not the case when Happy was sold at Sotheby's Auction House in London in September, 1989. Her price was 50 thousand pounds ($86 thousand). Happy was the first of the really shocking "record" bears. She was sold amid rumors about the royal family and rock stars. Another persistent story had her stuffed with cocaine! For over five years she retained the title "Most Expensive Bear in the World." At this writing, she is still the record holder in America. But this is not what really matters! Happy's price was never the most important thing to us. After we recovered from the shock, that is!

Because of her travels to meet people everywhere - and because of her efforts at raising monies for charities - Happy has become one of the most significant bears of the decade. Some call her an "icon." Happy gave a boost to the teddy bear business when it was at a low point. It has only gone up since then. According to newspaper reports, at the end of the 1990's the "plush" business amounts to over a billion dollars! And the greatest part is teddy bears.

We have become absolutely astounded at the feeling Happy Bear has evoked in people all over the world. Happy has meant many things to many people. She has been called the most beautiful bear in the world. In Germany they call her "Mona Lisa." People traveled hundreds of miles just to look at her! Many people have drawn a comparison between Happy and the late, beloved Princess of Wales. Both came from relative obscurity and were thrust into a glaring limelight. Both loved people - all kinds of people - and helped in any way possible. Both lost their titles but remained foremost in the hearts of the people who loved them. Now - we'd like to share Happy's story with you. We hope you enjoy it. It's all about love.

Happy's Story

For everyone who is Young at Heart

Once upon a time there was a sad little teddy bear.
She lived in the children's room of a big house in England.

Why was she so sad?

Well, for one thing, she had very big eyes.

Everyone kept saying - "Look! How funny!
I never saw a bear with big eyes like that!"

Actually, Happy couldn't see herself.
So she would never have known she was so different
if people hadn't kept on talking about it.

But she could see her fur.
It was lighter close to her body,
and quite brown on the ends.

Happy heard her owner say it was "tipped" fur.

She could tell by the way people replied,
"Oh," maybe this was not the best way to be.

Happy with the Big Eyes.

The other bears in the nursery were gold, beige, or white. And they all had eyes alike.

Happy heard people call their eyes "shoe button" eyes. Her's were only "different."

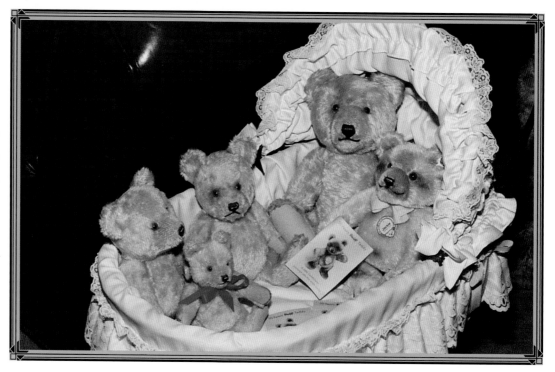

4

What hurt Happy most of all—the children got to play with the other bears, while *Happy was stuck on a high shelf.* The other bears had Easter tea parties with Peter Rabbit cups. They had English Breakfast tea and thin lemon cookies.

They had Farmhouse tea parties with a pig pitcher and a duck cream server and a pink pig sugar bowl. This was for ice cold milk and just out of the oven chocolate chip cookies. And Happy could only sit forlornly—watching and wishing she could play too!

At Christmas, the bears in the nursery got Santa caps and Christmas stockings. Their table was decorated with a chimney sweep to touch for good luck! Oh! How Happy wished she could touch him! But Happy got nothing. Forgotten on her shelf, she could only hum along to the music when they played Christmas Carols.

Another bear had a tulip tea set. Happy thought it probably held lemonade. She could just imagine how it tasted!

One of Happy's favorites was the cat and mouse tea set. She couldn't imagine the silly cat didn't know the mouse was on top of his head! She tried hard to imagine the taste of those caramel filled walnut cookies.

Happy longed to join the group playing the bumper car game. Those other bears had such jolly fun! They even invited the Billy Possum toy to join in!

7

Happy had to blink back tears when she watched the rough and ready pillow fights. Sometimes a loose feather would float up to her shelf. They were treasures! But the cleaning lady brushed them into her dust pan.

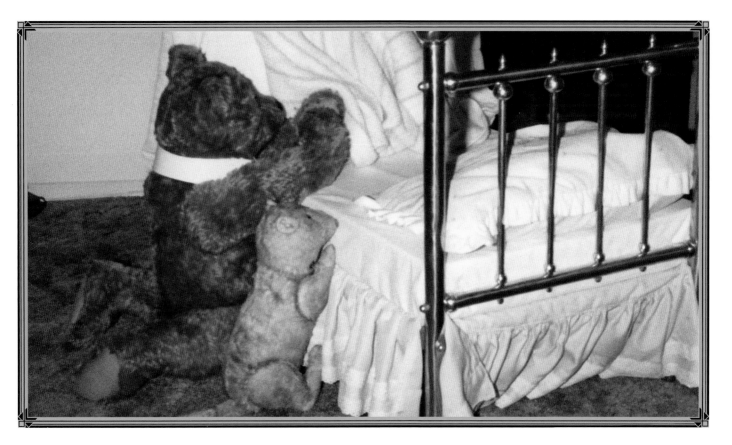

The other bears got to sleep in doll beds with doll bears of their own. When Happy said her prayers she asked for friends of her own and a bed. A family and love was her constant dream. A name would be nice, too.

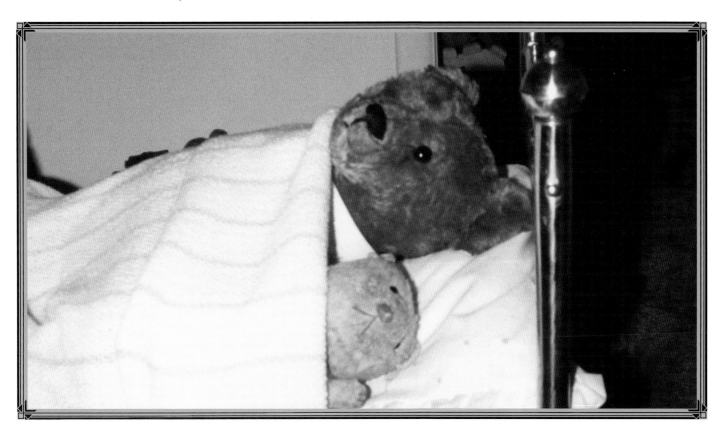

The other bears just read their stories and snuggled down in their warm blankets with their own tiny teds.

No one ever looked up to see the little bear with the big eyes looking down on them longingly.

Happy longed, with all her heart, to be able to look out the window and watch the children running and shouting with their bears, outside in the sun. She had to "just imagine."

Why was Happy stuck on a high shelf, just watching the fun?

She was the "Grand lady's" bear. The children were not allowed to play with her. She was a Steiff bear and cost too much for the children to cover with jam and kisses.

Happy hadn't asked to be the lady's bear. She would have chosen to play with the other bears and the children in the nursery. But sometimes you have to wait, patiently, for your turn. Sometimes it takes a very long time, and you almost give up. But Happy knew that if she was good and thought kindly about everyone, and was not mean and watched and learned, her turn would come! So she just sat there being good and patient, watching and learning. She thought oh! what a very long time it is taking! She almost gave up. And years went by.

The children in the nursery grew up and moved away. Their bears were packed away to save for the day when they had children of their own. The silence became almost unbearable for Happy. The nursery became a sewing room. When people did come in, which wasn't often, they never talked to Happy. They were too busy cutting, sewing and trying on clothes.

Finally, one quiet day, one of the boys, who had grown into a man, took Happy off her shelf and said, "Now that Mother is gone, I'm going to take this old bear to the auction house." At last! Happy was going to leave the sad old shelf! She was excited and scared! She wasn't sure what an "auction house" was, but she could hardly wait to see the things she had heard people talk about! For the first time ever she smelled hot dogs in the street push carts. She heard cars honking and people shouting and colored lights blinking on and off.

What a Wonderland!

When they got to that "auction house" the man filled out some papers and she went right back on a shelf!

"But I won't stop hoping," thought Happy with a shuddering sigh. And sure enough, in a few days a lady and a man came into the auction house and the lady asked to see "Lot 19" —which was the number on a tag tied around Happy's paw. Happy liked the lady!

The first thing the lady said was, "Oh! What beautiful eyes!" Happy was filled with excitement and hope! Someone **liked** her eyes! The lady said with a laugh, "And we both have tipped fur", so Happy thought her fur must not be that bad either.

Then the lady said, "May I hold her?" And Happy at last felt how it was to snuggle down in someone's arms and feel like you were really wanted and not "different." The lady was soft and warm and Happy could feel the lady's heart beating almost as fast as hers! This was what she had dreamed of! Reluctantly, with tears in her eyes (humans can cry, of course), the lady put Happy back on the counter.

Happy thought as hard as she could: *Don't leave me! Don't leave me!*

But the lady and man said, "We'll think about it," and left. The lady **had** heard Happy. Out on the sidewalk she said, "I think that bear was saying, 'Don't leave me.'" Poor Happy was back on a shelf with all the other bears who had no person to call their own. All she had left to hold on to was the smell of the lady's rose scented perfume. Happy wondered how long could one little bear keep on hoping?

A couple of days later, all the bears at the auction house were placed in boxes and there was a lot of excitement in the air. Today was the auction. When it was Happy's turn, she was frightened to look into such a sea of faces. The man with her kept yelling numbers and people raised their hands. Finally the man yelled, "Sold! Fifty thousand pounds," and hit the table hard. People were crowding around Happy and taking her picture and she was on television and she wasn't sure about this new world.

After the auction, she was packed carefully in a box and a nice lady (they called her a courier) rode with Happy across the ocean to the United States of America. The long hours wrapped in tissue and stuffed in a box were - what else could Happy call it - scary! But Happy was not one to complain. At least she tried not to!

When she was taken out of her box at Kennedy Airport can you ever guess who was there to meet her and give her a big hug and kiss?

Winnie the Pooh©—from Disneyworld!

Happy's friend, publisher Gary Ruddell, brought her roses.

To be out of the box, to be given roses, to actually **see** Winnie the Pooh,©

Happy thought she **must** be dreaming!

Is this the real Pooh?

Private bear talk.

Happy had listened carefully from her shelf as the lady read *Winnie the Pooh* stories to the children in the nursery. She could name all of Pooh's friends: Christopher Robin, Piglet, Owl, Eeyore, etc. Happy also shared Pooh's love of honey, like any other bear! So can you imagine the feeling of unreality - the absolute thrill to the bottom of her toe pads - when she got to **meet** Pooh? It remains one of the greatest thrills of this bear's life!!!

After another airplane ride, she finally was carried up a hill—her box was opened and miracle of miracles, there stood her lady and man from the auction house.

The man said, "Here's your anniversary present, babe."

The lady hugged her tightly and said, "Oh, thank you! I love her! We will name her Happy Anniversary and call her Happy for short!" Finally Happy had a name, a home, and love and lots of bear friends to be with. She was so glad she hadn't given up!

Meet some of Happy's new friends. It's easy to understand Happy had a great deal of catching up to do! She literally wanted to try everything! Some of her new friends were much older than she was. Edward (on the end) was made in 1903…23 years older than she.

Happy's friends taught her how to color in special books.

And ride a tricycle, after a fashion.

They taught her how to make chocolate chip cookies on the old wood stove in the corner of the kitchen. Being on the short side, Happy had to stand on pillows to reach the oven rack.

The first Christmas after she arrived, her lady's mother sewed her her own special stocking cap! Happy and her lady rang the bell to help the Salvation Army collect money for needy folk during the holy season.

Another Christmas, Happy's lady took her to the ballet to see "The Nutcracker"!

Now, **there** were things a bear could dream on! Tutus and tiaras! Sugar Plum Fairies! A Prince and Princess!

26

Nor did she have to hum along from her ceiling couch! She joined her very best and most constant friends, Bo and Dearheart, and they sang carols far into the night!

In days gone by, businesses and people stayed in the same location. Sometimes for generations! Now, Happy's friends all loved it on Buck Hill. When they were told they were going to move because of things called "smog" and "taxes", they were more than a little upset.

Until their hero, Edward, called to say he would take care of everything and it would be ALL RIGHT!

Edward was a cone nosed Steiff bear from the very early 1900's. He had been around a long time, and knew a great many things. His first chore was to take apart the computer system. Edward wasn't quite sure he had lived long enough for that!

When her family moved to Nevada, Happy put on her woolen stocking cap and raced around in the snowmobile! She had never imagined such fun!

Skiing was another favorite thing! Happy did a shuffle because her skis were antique and the poles had long ago been lost. But Happy figured shuffle skiing might just be best for a bear, anyhow.

When the snow melted and spring came, Happy tried to talk her way onto a Little League baseball team. She was told she was a few inches too short. But you know what? They let Happy keep the hat and sit in the stands and be the chief cheerleader. Wow! How she liked that!

Performing at a Blue Grass concert, Happy and her friend sing "Stand by Your Bear".

Happy, Bo, and Dearheart show their support for the troops of Desert Storm during the Gulf War. Happy has her own citizenship papers.

On a trip to Canada to help raise funds for the Alberta Children's Hospital, Happy and her lady met a real Royal Canadian Mounted Policeman!

On another trip to Buffalo, New York, Happy got to go in the place where they first made Buffalo wings. This trip was to help raise funds for the Teddy Roosevelt Inaugural site. Teddy Roosevelt is, quite naturally, her hero. Happy got to wear a very old campaign ribbon from when Roosevelt ran for President in 1904. It had a celluloid rose, and Happy was very, very careful!

Happy loves hats - even now. When they went to Australia to help friends Mike and Jackie Brooks raise money for the Camperdown Hospital, Happy's souvenir was an Aussie "fly away" hat. It's true you know, the corks bouncing around keep the flies away from your face.

You bet! Happy did! **And**, such a car! Silver, sleek, breathtaking! What happens when you adopt a car at the National Automobile Museum in Reno. Nevada, USA? You pay a fee and you get your name on a plaque in front of "your" car.

Then you attend a class on how to polish an antique auto properly. Four times a year you have to (or is it get to?) polish your car! Now that's exciting! Happy's car is a 1936 Mercedes Benz, type 500k Special Roadster by Daimler Benz. The original price was $10,750.00—at a time when a new Oldsmobile was around $500.00

When they traveled to Hennef, Germany for the Ciesliks' show, Happy sat quietly on a beautiful couch and greeted several thousand people. She thought "Ich bin Happy" was really funny and tried to remember it so she could tell her friends back home.

Happy was told this was the country of her origin. Her birth date was reckoned at 1926. But she had been sent early on to a store in England. That's how she became the Lady's bear and wound up on the nursery shelf. Actually, Happy had always been used to hearing English spoken, so she was pleased when her new people took her back to America - her people, her home, her friends!

She also liked the Indian headdress. She insisted she was a Chief Bear in this. It came in handy when she went to the Awaken Mother Earth Indian Pow Wow near her home in Nevada!

Do you believe in extra terrestrials? Happy does! And she was one of those lucky beings who got to attend the pre–opening day of the E.T. Ride on the Universal lot. She joined other patrons of the "Make–A–Wish Foundation". Proceeds went to Steven Spielberg's Starlight Pavilion Foundation.

On the other side of the city of Reno is an Air Base called "Stead". Once a year it hosts a National Air Race. The dry desert air and cloudless blue skies make it a perfect place for the competition of a variety of planes. A Grumman F8F-1 Bearcat seemed the way to go.

But Happy's first choice was "The Dragon Lady". It was an experimental plane built by a LADY– Pat Orcutt; who was also the pilot.

Happy's Paul (her lady's husband) inquired if he might put Happy on the wing to take a picture. The owner replied, "Sure you can. But why not put her in the cockpit?"

Happy thought she would surely pass out from sheer joy!

Probably Happy's sport of sports was croquet! She learned this at Amberly Castle in Sussex, England. The court had once been a moat, but had long since been drained. Happy and her people were in England to help raise money for Action Research.

Her lady took her to lots of places and people were always saying what made her so beautiful was her eyes! Oh, how things change! Happy got to go back to England to help raise money for little sick children. How she loved this! Being sick is a form of being different, she guessed.

She got to meet a princess,and ride on the Orient Express.

Michael Bond! The creator of Paddington Bear! She had seen Paddingtons of every size and color and description in the nursery! They were some of the Lady's children's favorites! When Happy actually saw Mr. Bond and heard him talk—and could tell what a genuine, fine human being he was, then she knew, being presented to a Princess can be even more precious when you are in line with Michael Bond, father of Paddington Bear!

At Amberley Castle in West Sussex, England, Happy found her Knight in Shining Armor.

46

Everywhere that she went, like here in Holland, the people loved her…and she loved them back.

Her new friends in Kyoto, Japan were so excited to see her that when the word got out she was in town, over 25,000 people came to see her.

They waited for hours in line at the Takashimaya Department Store, just to say "Hi!" to Happy.

A trip to Japan would not be complete without a trip to a shrine. What better way to travel than in a rickshaw?

49

Happy and the lady love each other very much.

Happy's dreams have most certainly come true!
She has her own name,
She lives in a house called Rose Cottage with a huge hug of bear friends and
She has her very own people who love her dearly!

Happy has felt blessed to have raised money for children's charities.
It made her feel good to "give back."

Her eyes, which had been so "different"
Are admired and copied all over the world!

Gratefully

Happy would like to say to every boy and girl
And to all you grown ups, too,
The shape of your eyes doesn't matter.
The color you are doesn't matter.
If your house is different, that doesn't matter.
What matters is that you
Dream your dreams,
Learn life's lessons,
Think good thoughts,
Practice kindness to everyone,
Be patient, patient, patient
Don't give up!
Then, according to Happy,
Your dreams can come true!